Learn to Share

Emma Dodd

Cartwheel
·B·O·O·K·S·®

Scholastic Inc.

**New York • Toronto • London • Auckland
Sydney • Mexico City • New Delhi • Hong Kong**

Dot and Dash are ready to play with their toys. Dot has a ball.

Dash wants to play with the ball.

But Dot does not want to share!

Dash has a truck.

**Big wants to play with the truck.
But Dash does not want to share!**

Dot has a doll.
Tall wants to play
with the doll.

But Dot does not want to share!

Dash has a teddy bear. Small wants to play with the teddy bear.

**Poor Teddy!
Time-out for
Dot and Dash!**

Dot and Dash are ready to play with their toys.

And this time, they are ready to share with their friends!

Dot and Dash
Fly a Kite

Dot and Dash are making a kite for their friends.

First Dot cuts some paper.

Dash is helping!

Next Dot needs some sticks.

Dash is helping!

Then Dot finds some string.

Dash is helping!
Now the kite is
almost ready. . . .

Uh-oh!
The kite is stuck.
What will Dot and Dash do now?

They need their friends to help them.
Tall is tall. Big is strong.
Small helps too!

Up goes the kite.
Hooray!

ISBN 978-0-545-23938-7

10 9 8 7 6 5 4 3 2 1   11 12 13 14/0

Printed in the U.S.A. 40

First American Edition, January 2011